THIS BOOK
BELONGS TO

This edition published by HarperCollins Publishers Ltd 1999 for Silverdale Books
An imprint of Bookmart Ltd
Registered Number 2372865
Trading as Bookmart Limited
Desford Rd, Enderby, Leicester, LE9 5AD
First published 1962 by Sampson Lowe
© Darrell Waters Limited 1962 as to all text and illustrations
Enid Blyton's signature mark and the word 'NODDY' are Registered
Trade Marks of Enid Blyton Ltd
All rights reserved
ISBN 0 26 167256-8
Printed and bound in Italy

NODDY AND THE TOOTLES

BY *Enid Blyton*

CONTENTS

SUDDENLY NODDY GAVE A SHOUT! "LOOK! THERE'S
A CARAVAN. I'M SURE IT'S MR TOOTLE'S"

1. THE TOOTLES

"COME along, little car," said Noddy, opening his garage doors. "Time to go out and do some work! It's *such* a lovely day!"

"Parp-parp!" said the little car, joyfully, and jiggled up and down. It was always pleased when Noddy came to fetch it from the dark garage.

Noddy gave it a quick polish with his big duster, and then out they both went into the sunshine. How nice and warm it was! Noddy bounced up and down in the driving seat, and began to sing.

The little car liked Noddy's singing. It joined in with a parp-parp whenever it could.

7

"Oh, isn't it fun
To be out in the sun,
Driving a dear little car!
PARP!
Wherever we go
There are people we know,
Thinking how lucky we are!
PARP!"

Noddy was singing so loudly that he didn't hear someone shouting at him. It was Mr Plod the policeman, standing in the middle of the road.

"NODDY! Slow down! What do you think you are—a fire-engine going to put out a fire? NODDY!"

"Oh—hallo, Mr Plod!" said Noddy, slowing down. "Was I really going fast? Ooooh, Mr Plod, I'd *love* to drive a fire-engine!"

"Well, the fire-engine wouldn't love it," said Mr Plod. "It would be shaken to pieces."

"PARP!" said the car, and almost ran over Mr Plod's big foot.

"Oh, sorry, Mr Plod," said Noddy. "The car didn't mean it. I must have taken off the brake. Oooh, look, Mr Plod—what's this coming down the street?"

Mr Plod turned to look. "Well, well, well!" he said. "It's a caravan, pulled by a horse—what a pace it's going! Hi there, slow down!"

The caravan was painted in lovely bright colours. It had four little windows, a door at the back and steps that could be lowered to the ground when the caravan stopped. There was a cheeky-looking little man driving it, dressed in a very bright shirt, a rather peculiar hat and red trousers.

He grinned as his caravan came up to Mr Plod and stopped. At once the door at the back opened, and a crowd of small children trooped down the steps shouting and laughing—goodness, what a lot there were! Their clothes were brightly coloured, but rather dirty and ragged. They raced over to Noddy's car at once, and one of them hooted the horn, making Mr Plod jump.

ONE OF THE CHILDREN HOOTED THE HORN,
MAKING MR PLOD JUMP

11

"Now—now—stop that!" he ordered.

"Oh, isn't it a lovely car?" said one of the girls. "Oh, I do like it! Oh, let me hold the steering-wheel, let me have a ride!"

Noddy rather liked the merry band of children, but Mr Plod didn't. "Move on, there, move on!" he ordered. Then he turned to the smiling caravan man. "Who are you, and where are you going?" he asked.

"I'm Mr Tootle," said the man, "and these children are my little Toots—Tommy Toot, Timmy Toot, Tilly Toot, Tabitha Toot . . ."

"All right, all right—that's enough!" said Mr Plod. "What do you do for a living?"

"Oh, I tootle," said Mr Tootle, and he sent one of the children into the caravan. Tommy Toot came back with a curious long thing that had holes all down it, and a mouth-piece.

"This is my tootle," said Mr Tootle. "Just you listen how I can play it!" He put it to his mouth and blew, moving his fingers over the holes as he did so — and out came a lovely whistling noise, clear as a black-bird's song. The tune was so merry and cheeky and loud that even Mr Plod's feet felt as if they wanted to dance in time to it!

"Hm!" said Mr Plod, trying to keep his feet still. "Funny way to earn money! Tootling like that. You'd better stop, Mr Tootle, you're causing a crowd, and that's not allowed."

Oh dear! Mr Tootle tootled so well that soon even Noddy's car was jiggling about in time to the tune, and Noddy was dancing on the pavement with all the caravan children! The Wobbly Man wobbled up, and soon he was wobbling to and fro in delight; and as for Miss Fluffy-Cat, Noddy had never seen her hopping and skipping about so gaily! Noddy couldn't help singing.

> "Oh, Mr Tootle's music
> Has flown into our feet,
> Look at us a-dancing
> Up and down the street,
> On and off the pavement,
> Jigging to and fro,
> Here we go a-dancing,
> Tippy-tappy toe!"

14

"What kind of music is that?" asked Mr Tubby Bear, coming up, and beginning to dance too, much to his surprise.

"It's called foot-music, sir," said Mr Tootle, stopping to get his breath. "Your feet hear it and dance."

"Now, move along, there, move along," said Mr Plod, sternly. "You can't cause a crowd like this, you know. Where are you going?"

"Nowhere," said Mr Tootle. "We just wander about from place to place. But as my wife is not well, I thought I'd find a nice field somewhere near here, and stay for a bit, till she's better."

"Oh. I'm *glad* you're staying!" said Noddy. "I do so like your tunes, Mr Tootle. And I like all your little Toots too—though I think that's a funny name for children!"

"You're a nice little chap!" said Mr Tootle, smiling all over his face at Noddy. "And you've a very nice little car—just the kind I'd like to pull my caravan for me, instead of a horse! I

15

suppose you don't know of a field we could go to, do you?"

"Oh *yes!*" said Noddy. "There's one at the bottom of my garden. Mr Plod, couldn't the Tootle family go there?"

"Certainly NOT!" said Mr Plod. "Caravans are not allowed in that field! Now move on, Mr Tootle, please, and take your caravan away."

"BUT . . ." began Mr Tootle, and stopped. Mr Plod had begun to look very fierce indeed. Mr Tootle nodded, gathered the little Toots around him, and marched them back to the caravan. They disappeared inside and shut the door. Mr Tootle climbed into the driving seat, and the horse pulled the caravan away down the street. They were gone!

16

2. THE CARAVAN IN THE FIELD

"I THINK you're rather unkind, Mr Plod," said Noddy. "I liked the Tootles."

"Now that's enough, Noddy," said Mr Plod. "I've heard about those Tootles before—they're up to all kinds of tricks. If Mr Tootle isn't a rogue, I'll eat my helmet!"

"Oh—*could* you eat your helmet, Mr Plod?" said Noddy, amazed. "Do just take a little bite at it and see if you can swallow it."

"I'll do nothing of the sort," said Mr Plod. "Will you PLEASE move on, Noddy? Haven't you any work to do this morning?"

Noddy drove off, thinking of the Tootles. What FUN to go round the country in a caravan pulled by a horse! What FUN to tootle merry dancing tunes for people to dance to! What FUN to have so many children laughing and playing together! Noddy suddenly felt rather lonely.

"I wish I had lots of brothers and sisters," he said, as he drove his car through the street, watching for passengers. "Still, I'm lucky to have Big-Ears and little Tessie Bear for friends. Oh, there's Mrs Tubby Bear with a heavy basket. Mrs Tubby, let me drive you home! I won't charge you even a penny because you made me such a lovely cake last week!"

Mrs Tubby Bear was very pleased. She climbed into the car, and put down her heavy basket. "You're a kind little fellow, Noddy," she said.

"Where's little Tubby Bear?" asked Noddy. "Have you left him at home?"

"Yes. He's been naughty again," said Mrs Tubby. "He put glue into Mr Tubby Bear's slippers, so of course poor Mr Tubby couldn't get them off last night, and had to sleep in his slippers."

"MRS TUBBY, LET ME DRIVE YOU HOME!"

19

Noddy thought that it was certainly a very naughty trick, but he couldn't help thinking it was funny too, and he gave a little giggle.

"Now you *know* you shouldn't laugh, Noddy," said Mrs Tubby. "Poor Mr Tubby—he really was upset. Well, here we are—and thank you very much."

Noddy was just about to go off again, when he saw something that surprised him. Whatever was that in the field at the bottom of his garden? His house was next door to Mrs Tubby's, so he could easily see the field. It couldn't be—no, surely it *couldn't* be Mr Tootle's caravan!

Noddy sat in his car, looking right down his garden into the field. As he sat there, little Tubby Bear came creeping out from under a bush. He waited till his mother was indoors, and then called excitedly to Noddy.

"Noddy! Look at that! A caravan in the field, and lots of children. We'll play with them and have fun. I've always wanted to see the inside of a caravan."

"Mr Plod said they weren't to go there," said Noddy. "I can't think why. There's not even a cow in that field now."

"Well, people oughtn't to waste a nice big field like that," said Tubby. "Noddy, there's a man there with a thing like a whistle, and he tootles on it. I wish he'd let me have a go."

"That's a tootle," said Noddy. "The man told me so himself. It's funny—his name is Mr Tootle, and he said that all his children were little Toots."

"I expect he made all that up just to sound funny," said Tubby. "Noddy—do let's go and see the caravan. Look, they've let the dear old horse loose—he's galloping round the field. We might have a ride on him."

"Well—we'll wait and see," said Noddy. Tubby had some good ideas, but they so often led to trouble that Noddy felt he had better be careful. After all, Mr Plod had said, very sternly, that Mr Tootle must NOT use that field, and he might come along at any time and turn the Tootles out. He would be cross to see Noddy and Tubby there.

22

"There's your mother calling you in for dinner," said Noddy. "You'd better go. I heard you were in disgrace, so you ought to be careful, Tubby. Whatever made you think of putting glue into your father's slippers?"

"Well, he said they were too big and kept slipping off his feet, so I thought glue would help to keep them on," said Tubby. "But I was scolded and then left behind this morning."

"Serves you right," said Noddy. "Well, I'm going to have *my* dinner, too. Oh, my goodness me— here's the Bumpy-Dog! Bumpy-Dog, go home! Why must you come just at dinner-time? I haven't enough for us both."

Bumpy-Dog was so pleased to see Noddy that he barked at the top of his voice, and then licked Noddy all over.

"All right, Bumpy—come in," said Noddy. "I can't bear you to stay outside and look sadly in at my window while I eat. You really are a dreadful dog. I can't think *why* I love you."

23

So Bumpy went into the House-For-One and shared Noddy's dinner. He ate most of it because he could eat much faster than Noddy. "You *gobble*, you don't *eat*," said Noddy. "Ooooh, listen—what's that?"

Bumpy-Dog cocked both his ears, put his head on one side and listened. Then he suddenly leapt up and began to prance about gaily—and Noddy found that he too was up and dancing all round the room.

"That's Mr Tootle's music again," said Noddy. "He plays foot-music, you know. It gets right into your feet! Oh, *don't* bump into me like that! Mr Tootle is in the field at the end of the garden, with a caravan. Oh, Bumpy—shall we go and see it?"

3. TEA WITH THE TOOTLES

WELL, that afternoon Noddy, Tubby and Bumpy-Dog all went over the wall at the back of Noddy's garden and into the field beyond. Mr Tootle's music seemed to call them.

"I've never heard such tunes before," said Noddy to Tubby. "Look, even Bumpy is dancing round like mad. I do wish I could tootle like that. I wonder if Mr Tootle would lend me his tootle just once!"

The caravan stood in the middle of the field, its steps leading down to the grass. The old horse was solemnly galloping round and round, with three of the little Toots on his back. A plump little woman was hanging out some washing on a line that stretched between two trees. Mr Tootle was sitting on an old box, tootling away merrily, whilst the rest of the little Toots leapt here and there in joy.

"It all looks very happy, doesn't it, Tubby?" said Noddy. "I'd like to live in a caravan, wouldn't you? A house on wheels that goes from place to place all the time! How lovely!"

Mrs Tootle saw them coming, and smiled at them. She didn't look as if she were ill, as Mr Tootle had said. She was fat and round, red-cheeked and smiling.

"Well, well, and who are you?" she said. "Have

you had your dinner? Would you like a chocolate biscuit? And what about this lovely dog of yours? Would he like a bone?"

"We've had our dinners," said Noddy. "But just the same, we'd like a chocolate biscuit, thank you very much."

All the little Toots gathered round them. "You're the driver of that nice little car we saw, aren't you?" said a small Toot. "Oooh, I do wish I could have a ride in it."

"Well I'm sure this nice little fellow will bring it into the field and let you each have a little ride," said Mrs Tootle. "He looks very kind."

Noddy was pleased that Mrs Tootle thought he was nice and kind, but he wasn't sure if he wanted to have all the little Toots riding in his car. But Tubby thought it was a fine idea. Perhaps Noddy might let *him* drive the car, just for once!

"Go on, Noddy—be kind!" he said. "Let's fetch your car and take these little Toots for

WHAT A TIME THOSE LITTLE TOOTS HAD!
THEY CLAMBERED ALL OVER THE CAR

a ride. I don't expect they've ever been in a car like yours. It can go so fast, too!"

"Can it? Can it?" asked all the little Toots, crowding round Noddy.

"Oh yes—very fast indeed," said Noddy proudly. "But I really don't know how I'd get it over the wall and into this field."

"Oh, just go round by the road, and come in at the field-gate, like we did," said a small Toot.

"All right," said Noddy. "I'll give you a treat. I won't be long!" And away he went across the field, over the wall, and into his garage. He drove his car round to the field-gate, and into the field, bumping over the rough clumps of grass.

Goodness me, what a time those little Toots had! They clambered all over the car, they hooted the horn, they pretended to drive. As for Bumpy, he nearly went mad with joy because he had so many people to play with!

But, oh dear, when three little Toots tumbled Noddy out of the car on to the grass, then climbed into the car themselves, and drove it round the field, Noddy was very angry.

"Don't do that!" he cried. "It's *my* car! No one is allowed to drive it but me! Oh, you naughty little things, you'll drive it into the ditch. Get out at once!"

But the little car did go into the ditch—and there it stuck, deep in the mud! Bumpy-Dog was angry with the little Toots and barked at them. They ran away, afraid, and called Mr Tootle from the caravan.

"Now, now, now, what's all the fuss?" said Mr Tootle. "Car in the ditch? Well, never mind. I'll get the man from the garage for you— he'll soon get it out! Go and have tea in the caravan—you must be hungry after playing all the afternoon!"

So Noddy, Tubby and Bumpy went to have tea in the caravan. It was great fun, and the tea was lovely. Noddy had never in his life seen so  many plates of cakes and biscuits! As for the Bumpy-Dog, he ate so many biscuits that he could hardly squeeze himself out of the caravan door!

"Hasn't the garage man come yet, to get my car out of the ditch?" asked Noddy, wishing he hadn't eaten quite so many cakes.

"Er—no. He said he'd come round to the field first thing tomorrow morning," said Mr Tootle, getting out his whistle. "I'll play a few tunes for you all, just to shake down your tea!"

And, goodness me, you should have seen Noddy, Tubby, Bumpy and all the Tootle children, dancing round the field in time to the merry tunes coming out of the big tootle. Noddy was tired, and wanted to stop, but he couldn't. At last his feet wouldn't dance any more, and he felt very sleepy. So did Tubby. As for Bumpy, he was sound asleep in the caravan!

"I'll have to go home," Noddy told Mrs Tootle. "Thank you for a lovely time. I wish I had a tootle like your husband's. I'll come for my car tomorrow morning when the garage man has pulled it out of the ditch. Goodbye!"

And away they went, yawning. The Tootle children called goodnight, and waved. It had been great fun — but oh, Noddy did wish his dear little car was safely in its garage.

"It won't like being all alone in a muddy ditch all night," he told Tubby Bear. "It will be very lonely."

"If it hoots for you, you won't hear it," said Tubby, and Noddy felt sadder still. Then he heard Mrs Tubby Bear calling Tubby in a very cross voice and he hurried into his little House-For-One with Bumpy-Dog. Tubby was going to get into trouble again, that was certain — and

32

Mrs Tubby might give Noddy a scolding, too!

"You'd better go home quickly to Tessie Bear," Noddy said to the Bumpy-Dog. "Or *you'll* get into trouble too, for being out so long. Oh dear—I hope Mr Plod doesn't hear that the Tootle family are in the field he said they weren't to go to—and that I went to play with them. I think perhaps it was rather silly of me. Oh, my poor little car! Don't be lonely and cold all by yourself in the ditch. I'll fetch you tomorrow morning, just as soon as ever I can!"

4. A SHOCK FOR LITTLE NODDY

NODDY woke up late the next morning. He sat up at once and looked at his clock. "Oh dear, I'm late—and my little car must be waiting for me out in the field. I danced too much yesterday—I'm tired!"

He dressed quickly, ran down his garden, and was just climbing over the wall into the field when he had a dreadful shock.

The caravan was gone! Not a single one of the Tootle family was to be seen! And oh what a dreadful thing—Noddy's car was gone too! The ditch was empty! Only the old horse was left, looking rather lonely. He came trotting up to Noddy and put his long nose on Noddy's shoulder.

"Horse! Where has Mr Tootle's caravan gone? Where is everyone? And where, oh where is my car?" wailed Noddy. "Oh, that horrid Mr Tootle—I *know* what he's done! He has tied my car to the front of his caravan, and driven it out of the field—and goodness knows where they are now! My poor little car! Oh why did I ever go to see the Tootles yesterday?"

"Hrrrrrrumph!" said the horse, very sadly, and looked at Noddy out of big brown eyes.

"Poor horse! They've left you here alone! Oh, what horrid people they are—and I thought they were so nice! I'm very, very sorry about it, horse."

"Hrrrrrumph!" said the horse again, and two big tears rolled out of his eyes and trickled down Noddy's neck. Noddy was very upset. He put his arms round the horse's neck and spoke kindly to him. "Don't cry.  You can have this field till we find the Tootles. I'll bring you lumps of sugar. I'll be your friend."

"HRRRRRRUMPH!" said the horse, so very loudly that Noddy almost fell over. "I must go and find Mr Plod," he told the horse. "I'll be back soon."

Well, Mr Plod listened to Noddy's story, and shook his head solemnly. "I *told* you they would be up to tricks. I told you they weren't to be allowed in that field. I knew they would do something bad. And so they have."

"But Mr Plod, they've *taken my car*, I keep telling you. And I want it back," said Noddy, crying big tears down his front. "Won't you go after them, please?"

"I don't know where they've gone," said Mr Plod. "And if you think I'm going all over the country trying to find those Tootles, you're  wrong. You should have listened to what I said. If your car is gone for ever, it's your own fault. Those Tootles probably hitched it to their caravan in the middle of the night and off they went, tootling away! Perhaps you'll take notice of what I say next time, Noddy."

"Oh, Mr Plod, I will, I will," wept Noddy. "I'll go and tell Big-Ears. Whatever shall I do without my car to take people about in? I shan't be able to earn any money. I shall starve, I . . ."

"BUT MR PLOD, THEY'VE TAKEN MY CAR," SAID NODDY,
CRYING BIG TEARS

37

"Well, when people do silly things, it's their own fault," said Mr Plod. "Go and see Big-Ears, and don't bother me any more."

So off went poor Noddy to find Big-Ears the brownie, walking all the way through the wood to Toadstool House, where Big-Ears lived. Big-Ears was *most* surprised to see Noddy looking so miserable.

Soon Noddy had told him all about the Tootles, and how they had taken his car, and left behind the dear old horse. Big-Ears listened without a word, shaking his head every now and again. Then he put his arm round Noddy and gave him a very comfort-ing hug.

"Poor little Noddy! I won't scold you! You are sad enough as it is. But Mr Plod is right — no-body knows where those Tootles are, and it's no good looking for them. You'll just have to hope that your little car will escape from them one day and come home to you. They *might* forget to tie it to the caravan sometime."

38

"But how shall I take people about? How shall I carry their shopping?" wept Noddy.

"Well, you'll just have to use that nice old horse the Tootles left behind," said Big-Ears. "You can ride him—and he will be big enough to take packages and parcels. You can be a parcel-postman—delivering all kinds of things to people's houses. Tuppence a time."

"But will the horse like that?" asked Noddy, wiping his eyes.

"Well, it will be easier work for him than dragging a heavy caravan," said Big-Ears. "You go back and catch the horse, and tell him you'll be his master now, and that you'll be very kind to him. I'm sure he'll like you."

"He likes me already," said Noddy. "Well, I'll go now. And don't forget, Big-Ears, I'll carry your parcels and packages anywhere you like — on horseback now!"

And off he went, feeling a bit more cheerful. He even managed to sing a little song, though it was in rather a sad voice.

"I haven't a car, I've a horse instead,
 With eyes that are soft and brown,
 And we'll carry the parcels and packages too,
 A-galloping up and down!
 Off we will go on our trit-trotting feet,
 Delivering packages all down the street!
 Hhruumph, hhruumph, HHRUUMPH!"

40

5. NODDY AND THE HORSE

NODDY told everyone about the horse, and how his dear little car had been stolen to pull the Tootles' caravan, and they were all very sorry.

Bumpy-Dog was so sad about it that he trotted all the way from Tessie Bear's with a most enormous bone in his mouth, to give Noddy for his dinner. All the dogs in the town followed him, of course, and Noddy was MOST astonished to see Bumpy with a long, long line of all kinds of dogs behind him.

They all came trotting into Noddy's garden, and he had a dreadful time trying to make them go away. "Bumpy, it was kind of you to think of me," he said. "But it's rather a smelly bone, so please do take it away—and take all those dogs too. They're spoiling my garden."

So away trotted Bumpy again, very disappointed, with all the dogs frisking after him. Really—*what* a dog!

"Now I'll go and fetch that horse," said Noddy. So off he went, climbing over his garden wall into the field. The horse galloped up at once, and put his head on Noddy's shoulder again. Then he suddenly sneezed, and it was such an enormous sneeze that poor Noddy was blown right off his feet.

"Good gracious, horse— what a cold you've got!" said Noddy. "You should sneeze into a hanky, not all over *me*. I haven't one big enough for you, though — you'd need a tablecloth, to catch one of *your* sneezes!"

The horse gave a funny little whinnying noise as if to say "You really are a kind little fellow!" Noddy stroked the long nose, and told the horse what he was planning to do.

"I want you to take me round the town to collect parcels and packages," he said. "I shall charge people tuppence a time. Come along to the gate and we'll go."

Noddy climbed on to the horse's back. It was rather slippery. He had to hold on to the horse's mane as they trotted along, to stop himself from falling off. It really was rather a big horse.

The horse didn't behave very well on the way to

town. He kept seeing delicious-looking new leaves on the trees they passed, and stood up on his hind legs to nibble them.

"I do wish you wouldn't do that, horse," said Noddy. "That's the third time I've slipped all the way down your back and on to the ground. Please don't stand up on your hind legs any more."

Then, just as the horse reached the busy cross-roads, where Mr Plod stood, he gave another sneeze—a most tremendous one. It blew off Mr Plod's helmet, which went rolling along the road, and Noddy fell off again.

"Is this the horse I've heard about, Noddy?" said Mr Plod. "Well, I don't think much of him, sneezing my helmet off my head! Go and pick it up, please, before a car runs over it."

The horse thought he would run after the helmet too, and alas, just at that very moment Big-Ears came along on his bicycle—and he and the horse ran into one another!

CRASH! Over went Big-Ears, and everyone began

to shout loudly. "Catch that horse! Catch it! CATCH THAT HORSE!"

The horse gave another sneeze and sat down firmly on Big-Ears' bicycle. Big-Ears was so angry that he could hardly speak. He stood up and shook his fist at the horse, who thought Big-Ears was having a kind of game. He put down his head and ran at Big-Ears, his tail waving merrily in the air. Down went poor Big-Ears again!

"Lock up that horse!" shouted Big-Ears to Mr Plod. "He's dangerous! Put him in prison!"

The horse was so scared to hear this that he kicked up his heels, whisked his tail, and galloped up the road at top speed, sneezing as he went. "Clippitty-clop, a-TISH-oo, clippitty-clop, a-TISH-oo!"

"Oh, my horse has gone!" wailed Noddy. "You've scared him, Big-Ears. Now I can't take parcels and packages for anyone."

"You said he was a *nice* horse, and he isn't," said

Big-Ears, picking up his bicycle, and trying to straighten a bent pedal. "Good thing he's gone, I say."

"All the same, I did like him," said Noddy. "NOW what am I going to do? Oh, I *wish* I had my dear little car. Oh, I'm so unhappy without it. I'm trying to be brave, Big-Ears, I really am."

"I should think that horse has gone to find the caravan," said Big-Ears. "What about following him on my bicycle?"

"Oh *yes*, Big-Ears!" said Noddy. "That's a very, very good idea!" So off they went, and Big-Ears sang a loud song as the bicycle went along, with Noddy sitting behind.

"Has anyone seen a galloping horse,
 A horse with a terrible sneeze,
 And four strong legs and a tail, of course,
 Has anyone seen him, PLEASE?"

6. WHERE ARE THOSE TOOTLES?

QUITE a lot of people had seen the horse, and pointed out the way he had gone. "Up there, look—he nearly blew me off my feet when he sneezed," said a little monkey. "He ought to be in bed with a cold like that!"

"Along that lane he went, and over the bridge," said a farmer. "Never saw a horse go so fast in my life!"

Noddy sat on the back of Big-Ears' bicycle and held on tight. Would the horse find the Tootles' caravan? Was he clever enough?

Up and down the hills went the bicycle, with Big-Ears ringing his bell loudly at every corner, and stopping every now and then to ask if the horse had gone by that way. And then suddenly Noddy

"ALONG THAT LANE HE WENT, AND OVER THE
BRIDGE," SAID A FARMER

gave a loud shout.

"LOOK! There's a caravan. I'm sure it's Mr Tootle's. I'm sure it is. On that hill there, look!"

And sure enough it was! It stood there quietly in the big field, with all the little Toots playing round! Noddy was so very pleased. "Now we can get my car back!" he said.

Big-Ears jumped off his bicycle and began to walk, because the hill was so steep. He stared

at the caravan, and then turned to Noddy. "Can you see your car? I can't."

"No. No, I can't," said Noddy, looking hard. "What have they done with it? Oh, Big-Ears—surely they haven't sold it!"

"We'll soon see," said Big-Ears, in a very stern voice. He wheeled his bicycle through a

48

gate and went up to the caravan with Noddy. The little Toots swarmed round them, pleased to see Noddy again.

"Where's my car?" asked Noddy at once.

"Mr Tootle has gone shopping in it," said Mrs Tootle, beaming at Noddy and Big-Ears. "I hope you don't mind us borrowing it, Noddy."

"You didn't borrow it. You *stole* it," said Big-Ears. "And I am sending Mr Plod the policeman up here to arrest Mr Tootle and take him to prison."

"But you've got our horse," said Mrs Tootle. "That's a fair exchange, isn't it? Noddy said we could have his car if we gave him our horse."

"Oh, what a story!" said Noddy, shocked. "Oh, what a DREADFUL story! As if I would give my car away to anyone!"

"Well, here comes Mr Tootle now," said Mrs Tootle. "He'll soon tell your friend that you said you'd exchange your car for our horse."

And sure enough, there was Mr Tootle driving Noddy's car into the field! It was piled so high with

49

shopping that Noddy could hardly see him!

"My car! My dear litle car!" yelled Noddy —and at once the car ran straight over the field to him, saying "Parp-parp-parp-parp-parp!" without stopping. It ran so fast that half the parcels fell out, and Mr Tootle had a terrible bumping.

Noddy patted the car's bonnet and glared fiercely at Mr Tootle, who was smiling broadly at him. "Hallo, hallo!" he said. "Here's my little friend Noddy, again. How do you do? It was so nice of you to exchange your car for my horse. It's a good little car. How's the horse?"

"MY CAR! MY DEAR LITTLE CAR!" YELLED NODDY—
AND AT ONCE THE CAR RAN STRAIGHT TO HIM

51

"You bad man!" cried Noddy. "I DIDN'T exchange my car. I wouldn't dream of doing such a thing. I love my car very much. Give it back to me at once."

"You'd better do what Noddy says, Mr Tootle," said Big-Ears, very sternly. "Or Mr Plod will be up here in no time."

"Well, well, well — if little Noddy really wants his car back, he shall have it," said Mr Tootle. "But only if he gives me back my horse. Fair's fair, you know. I MUST have something to pull my caravan."

He jumped out of the car, still smiling, and took up his tootle, which lay beside him on the seat. He put it to his lips and began to tootle. And, oh dear, it was that lovely foot-music again!

Big-Ears frowned. "Stop that! This is no time to whistle and tootle. Get away from that car and let Noddy get in."

But before he had finished speaking his feet had begun to dance! How they danced! They kicked and clicked and tapped and stamped and he simply couldn't stop them! Noddy was dancing too, with three of the little Tootles in a ring. Mrs Tootle stood by, laughing.

Mr Tootle stopped for breath. He shouted to Noddy. "Give me back my horse, and I promise you shall have your car!"

"The horse ran away. I haven't got it!" yelled Noddy.

"Well, that's too bad!" said Mr Tootle. "You can't have your car then—no horse, no car!" And he lifted his tootle to his mouth again.

But somebody else had heard Mr Tootle's merry whistling—somebody who was galloping up the hill—somebody who pushed through the gate, and gave such a very loud sneeze that all the dancers swung round in surprise!

"It's the HORSE!" yelled Noddy. "He heard you tootling—it's the HORSE! Now I can have my car back!"

7. NODDY IS HAPPY AGAIN!

SURE enough, it *was* the horse! When he saw the Tootles he raced across the field and nuzzled round every one of them. The little Toots were pleased—they had missed him very much. But Mr Tootle was angry with the horse.

"Of course you *would* come back at the wrong moment—with one of your bad colds too!"

"A-WHOOOSHOOO!" sneezed the horse, and it was such a big sneeze that two of the little Toots were blown right over. The horse trotted to the front of the caravan and stood there as if he were waiting to be hitched on to it. Noddy ran to him and patted his nose.

"Oh *thank* you for coming back! Now I shall have my car again. I do like you, horse, even though you weren't any help to me. I'm glad you wanted to come back to the Tootles, though Mr Tootle isn't a nice man at all."

"He certainly isn't," said Big-Ears, glaring at Mr Tootle. "He can't even say he's sorry. Just wait till Mr Plod hears all this!"

"We shall be miles away by tomorrow," said Mr Tootle. "He won't be able to find us. Ah well—I enjoyed driving that nice little car. I'll just go and take out the rest of my parcels, and then this little nodding fellow can drive it away. Let's give him a sugar bun—he looks hungry."

And there was Noddy, munching a most delicious sugar bun, and helping Mr Tootle and the little Toots to empty his car of parcels! Big-Ears stood nearby and scowled.

"I think I'd better tootle again," said Mr Tootle to Big-Ears. "You look cross, and a little more dancing will do you good."

"I think you ought to *pay* Noddy for using his car like that," said Big-Ears. "You're a rogue, Mr Tootle, and I don't like you."

"Well, I don't like *you* very much either," said Mr Tootle. "Where are you going, Noddy?"

Noddy was running over to the caravan, where the horse still stood patiently waiting to be hitched. He put his arms around the horse's neck.

"I hope you'll be happy," he said. "Run away to me if you aren't. Goodbye, dear horse."

The horse butted Noddy gently with its nose, as if to say "Goodbye" too. Then it gave a loud "HHRRRUMMPH" and an even louder "AWHOOSHOO" sneeze, and away flew Noddy's hat over the field, its bell tinkling as it went!

"Noddy! Hurry up! Your car's ready to go!" shouted Big-Ears, and the little car hooted impatiently. "Parp-parp-PARP!"

Noddy ran over to it gladly, and jumped into the driving-seat. Big-Ears was already in the car, still glaring at Mr Tootle. He had put his bicycle at the back. Noddy shouted to all the Tootles as they went.

"NODDY! HURRY UP! YOUR CAR'S READY TO GO!"
SHOUTED BIG-EARS

"Goodbye, all you Tootles,
And please don't forget
To love the old horse,
He *is* such a pet!
Don't work him too hard,
Give him plenty of hay.
Goodbye, all you Tootles,
We're off and away!"

"Fancy wasting a nice little song like that on the
Tootles," said Big-Ears grumpily, as the little car
drove happily out of the field on to the road. "That
horrid, grinning Mr Tootle! He ought to have *paid*
you for the use of your car. He didn't give you even
a penny!"

"What's that rattling noise, Big-Ears?" said
Noddy suddenly, turning his head round. "I do
hope there's not anything wrong with the car."

"Sounds like something jiggling about at the
back," said Big-Ears. "A bit of Mr Tootle's
shopping, I should think. Get out and look,
Noddy."

Noddy jumped out and looked in the back of the car. Then he gave a loud shout of joy. "BIG-EARS! What do you think Mr Tootle has left here for me? Oh, Big-Ears, guess!"

"*I* don't know," said Big-Ears.

"He's put a *tootle* in here for me!" cried Noddy. "Look—a little tootle, just like his big one that plays that lovely music. Oh, BIG-EARS, I shall be able to play foot-music, too. Listen!"

And Noddy put it to his mouth and tootled away—and Big-Ears' feet at once began to wriggle and tap on the car's floor. He couldn't help smiling.

"Well, well, well—so you've a tootle now! I can see that we are going to have some funny times in Toy Town, Noddy. Wait till Mr Plod hears your tootle—ho, ho, ho, what a sight that will be, to see Mr Plod dancing round in the street! Ah well— I suppose it's Mr Tootle's way of paying you for the use of your car!"

Noddy put the tootle away safely, and went back to the driving-seat, smiling all over his face. A tootle—a tootle all of his own! He'd have Tessie Bear dancing all over the place—and Bumpy-Dog—and Mr Tubby Bear—oooh, what a fine time he was going to have! He sang loudly to Big-Ears.

> "Oh, I've a fine tootle,
> And when I've the chance
> I'll blow it and blow it
> And make you all dance!
> Off you'll go jigging
> On two happy feet,
> Tapping and tripping
> Away down the street!"

Dear me, Noddy, what a time you will have with your tootle. Do go and play it to Mr Plod!